Andy Pandy Storybook

Illustrations by Anne Matthews

Contents

A catalogue record for this book is available from the British Library.

First edition

Published by Ladybird Books Ltd Loughborough Leicestershire UK
Ladybird Books Inc Auburn Maine 04210 USA

Andy Pandy © 1951 Freda Lingstrom
Flowerpot Men © 1953 Freda Lingstrom
Licensed by BBC Enterprises Limited
© In presentation LADYBIRD BOOKS LTD MCMXCI

Printed in England (3)

Andy Pandy
paints
a picture

Andy Pandy and Teddy went into the garden to pick flowers for Looby Loo, but it started to rain and they had to run back into the house.

"We will have to paint a picture of flowers for her," said Andy Pandy.

They fetched the paint pots from the cupboard and started to paint.

Teddy found it very difficult to paint with a brush so he used his paws instead. First he put them into the yellow paint, then into the red, then back into the yellow, so the paints got all mixed up together.

"You must wipe your paws when you change colours," said Andy Pandy.

Teddy started again.

He painted a yellow flower, and he wiped his paws down his tummy.

Then he painted a red flower, and wiped his paws again.

Then he painted some green leaves, and this time, he wiped his paws behind his ears.

"Just look at you," cried Andy Pandy. "You're covered in paint!"

Teddy laughed, and ran round
and round the room singing,

*"I'm the brightest little bear
  you ever did see.
Look what the paint has
  done to me.
Yellow, red, green and blue,
Now you can see
  what paint will do."*

"It's a good thing it's the kind of paint that will wash off," said Andy Pandy, "or you would have to stay like that."

Teddy started to wipe the paint off with a cloth. "No not like that!" cried Andy.

"You must wash it off. The only thing to do is to put you in the bath."

Teddy didn't like baths. He ran round and round the room and out into the garden so that Andy Pandy couldn't catch him. Very soon there were patches of paint everywhere.

When Andy Pandy caught Teddy he put him straight in the bath. "Be good while I go and clean up all the mess," he said crossly.

Teddy had to scrub very hard to wash away all the paint, and when he had finished he sang,

"I'm the cleanest little bear
you ever did see.
Look what a bath has done to me.
Green and yellow, blue and red,
I must stay clean
till it's time for bed."

Andy Pandy cleaned away all the paint patches, and took a big towel to dry Teddy. But Teddy had got out of the bath and was shaking himself dry. Water was flying everywhere!

"Look what you've done!" cried Andy. "Now I'll have to clean up this mess, too!"

"I'm sorry," said Teddy, shamefully. "I'll help this time. I won't do it again, I promise."

Head, shoulders, knees and toes

Head, shoulders,
*   knees and toes,*
*   knees and toes,*
Head, shoulders,
*   knees and toes,*
*   knees and toes,*
And eyes and ears
*   and mouth and nose,*
Head, shoulders,
*   knees and toes,*
*   knees and toes.*

Andy Pandy and Teddy are singing a song. Do the actions with them.

Bill and Ben
and the
nut store

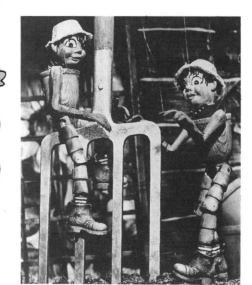

One day, when the man who works in the garden had gone home, Bill and Ben the Flowerpot Men climbed out of their flowerpots. The wind was blowing very hard, and it blew off their hats.

They ran after them, but the wind blew their hats into a big flower bush. And it took Bill and Ben a long time to find them.

While they were away, a squirrel who was playing in the garden said to himself, "I wonder what Bill and Ben keep in their flowerpots? I'll go and have a look."

He climbed into Bill's flowerpot. It was empty.

He climbed into Ben's flowerpot, and that was empty, too.

"Oh, dear me!" said the squirrel. "Bill and Ben haven't any nuts stored up for the winter. Whatever will they do when it snows?" And he ran off to tell them that they must gather some nuts.

But the squirrel couldn't find Bill and Ben. They were inside the big flower bush, looking for their hats.

Can you see them?

"It will snow soon," thought the squirrel to himself. "I must help Bill and Ben." And he went to the bottom of an old tree and dug up some of the nuts he had hidden for himself.

He put some of the nuts in Bill's flowerpot and some in Ben's. Then he ran to the big oak tree, gathered some acorns and carried them to the flowerpots.

By the time Bill and Ben had found their hats they were quite tired, and they went back to their flowerpots to have a rest.

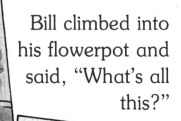

Bill climbed into his flowerpot and said, "What's all this?"

Ben climbed into his flowerpot and said, "What have we here?"

"There are nuts and acorns in my flowerpot," called out Bill.

"I've got some in mine, too," called Ben.

Then they both said, "I wonder who put them there?"

"I put them there," said the squirrel. "I'm very pleased to see you back. I was quite worried when I found that you wouldn't have anything to eat when it snows."

"You are very kind," said Bill.

"That was very nice of you," said Ben.

And they both said, "Thank you very much."

The squirrel hurried away to find more nuts for his store.

When he had gone, Bill and Ben climbed out of their flowerpots. "It really was very kind of him," said Bill. "The nuts will be useful but we can't eat acorns."

"I know what we'll do with them," said Ben. "We'll plant them. One day they might grow into big oak trees."

And that is what they did.

How many blue things can you see in the picture?

Who has been painting?
Was it Bill or was it Ben?